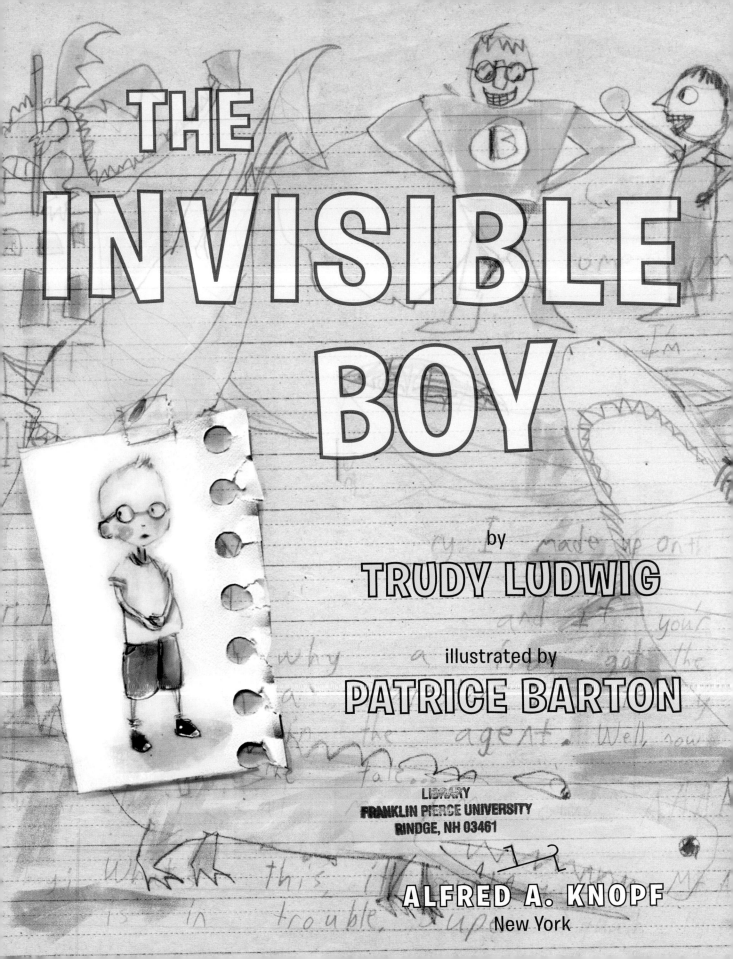

THE INVISIBLE BOY

by

TRUDY LUDWIG

illustrated by

PATRICE BARTON

ALFRED A. KNOPF
New York

Can you see Brian, the invisible boy? Even Mrs. Carlotti has trouble noticing him in her classroom. She's too busy dealing with Nathan and Sophie.

Nathan has problems with what Mrs. Carlotti calls "volume control." He uses his outside voice inside too much.

Sophie whines and complains when she doesn't get her way.

Nathan and Sophie take up a lot of space. Brian doesn't.

When the bell rings for recess, Micah and J.T.
take turns choosing kids for their kickball teams.

The best players get picked first.

Then the best friends of the best players.

Then the friends of the best friends.

Only Brian is left, still waiting and hoping.

J.T. glances in Brian's direction and, just as quickly, looks away. "We've got enough players for each team," he tells the others. "Let's play ball!"

In the cafeteria, Madison and her friends talk about her birthday party.

"The rope swing over the pool was awesome!" says J.T.

"Yeah, so was the waterslide," adds Fiona.

"That was the best pool party ever!"

"I'm so glad you guys had fun!" says
Madison. Everybody did except Brian.
He wasn't invited.

At Choosing Time, while the other kids play board games
and read, Brian sits at his table, doing what he loves to do best:
He draws fire-breathing dragons scaling tall buildings . . .

. . . space aliens locked in
intergalactic battles . . .

. . . greedy pirates
digging for treasure . . .

. . . and superheroes with
the power to make friends
wherever they go.

On Monday morning, Mrs. Carlotti introduces
Justin, a new student, to the class. Brian smiles shyly
at him. Some of the other kids sneak looks at Justin,
trying to figure out if he's cool enough to be their
friend. They haven't quite made up their minds yet.

At lunch, Madison and J.T. watch Justin eat with chopsticks. "What's *that*?" asks Madison as she points at Justin's food.

And the kids laugh. All of them, that is, except Brian. He sits there wondering which is worse—being laughed at or feeling invisible.

At morning recess, Brian finds a piece of
chalk on the ground and starts drawing away.

"Hey, Justin," Emilio calls out from the tetherball court, "you're up next."

"Sorry, I gotta go," says Justin. "By the way, that's a really cool drawing," he adds before taking off.

Back in class, Mrs. Carlotti asks the kids to team up in twos or threes for a special project. The kids scurry around the room to pair off. Brian heads toward Justin.

"I'm already with Justin," says Emilio.
"Find someone else."

Brian looks at the floor, wishing he could draw a hole right there to swallow him up.

Mrs. Carlotti gives the class directions for the project.
"Your assignment is to work together to write a story about
what you see in that photograph."

"Whoa . . . cool!" says Emilio. "What kind of people do you think would live in houses like that?"

"I don't know, but I bet Brian could draw them to go with our story," says Justin.

Brian smiles as he takes out his lucky pen.

Some crooked story We made up on the spot

Narrator: Hi, I'm the narrator and if you're wondering why a pirate got the part of a Narrator I'll tell you. It's all in the agent. Well now on with the tale...

The crooked story we made up on the spot

It's lunchtime again—Brian's least favorite part of the day.
Another twenty l-o-n-g minutes of kids talking and laughing
with everyone else . . . but him.

"Brian!" he hears someone shout. "Hey, Brian—over here!"

Brian turns and sees Justin waving him over. Emilio
nods at Brian as he makes room for him at the table.

Maybe, just maybe, Brian's not so invisible after all.

QUESTIONS FOR DISCUSSION

When the bell rings for recess, Micah and J.T. take turns choosing kids for their kickball teams.

- How did Micah and J.T. choose players for their teams? Was it a fair way to select players? Why or why not?
- Have you ever tried to join a group, game, or activity and other kids wouldn't let you? If yes, how did that make you feel?
- Have you ever intentionally excluded other kids from joining your group, game, or activity? If yes, why?

"I'm so glad you guys had fun!" says Madison. Everybody did except Brian. He wasn't invited.

- When Madison and her friends talked about her birthday party in front of Brian, do you think they were just being thoughtless or were they being mean to Brian on purpose? Explain.
- Was there a better way for Madison to handle the situation when she and her friends started to talk about her party in front of those kids who weren't invited?
- Have you ever found yourself in a similar situation as Brian, with kids talking about the fun things they've done with each other in front of you and you weren't included or invited? If yes, how did that make you feel?

He sits there wondering which is worse—being laughed at or feeling invisible.

- How many examples in this story can you find that show Brian's invisibility?
- Which do you think is worse—being laughed at or feeling invisible? Explain.
- What did Brian do to help Justin feel better after J.T. and the other kids made fun of the food he was eating?

Maybe, just maybe, Brian's not so invisible after all.

- How many kids did it take in this story to help Brian begin to feel less invisible?
- What specifically did Justin do to make Brian feel less invisible?
- Are there kids in your class, grade, or school who you see being treated as if they are invisible? If yes, what could you do to make them feel more valued and appreciated?

RECOMMENDED READING FOR ADULTS

Borba, Michele, EdD. *Nobody Likes Me, Everybody Hates Me: The Top 25 Friendship Problems and How to Solve Them.* San Francisco: Jossey-Bass, 2005.

Cain, Susan. *Quiet: The Power of Introverts in a World That Can't Stop Talking.* New York: Crown, 2012.

Elman, Natalie Madorsky, PhD, and Eileen Kennedy-Moore, PhD. *The Unwritten Rules of Friendship: Simple Strategies to Help Your Child Make Friends.* New York: Little, Brown and Company, 2003.

Rubin, Kenneth H., PhD, and Andrea Thompson. *The Friendship Factor: Helping Our Children Navigate Their Social World—and Why It Matters for Their Success and Happiness.* New York: Viking, 2002.

Thompson, Michael, PhD, Catherine O'Neill Grace, and Lawrence J. Cohen, PhD. *Best Friends, Worst Enemies: Understanding the Social Lives of Children.* New York: Ballantine Books, 2002.

RECOMMENDED READING FOR KIDS

Button, Lana. *Willow's Whispers.* Tonawanda, NY: Kids Can Press Ltd., 2010.

Cave, Kathryn. *Something Else.* New York: Mondo Publishing, 1998.

Cooper, Scott. *Speak Up and Get Along!: Learn the Mighty Might, Thought Chop, and More Tools to Make Friends, Stop Teasing, and Feel Good About Yourself.* Minneapolis: Free Spirit, 2005.

Lovell, Patty. *Stand Tall, Molly Lou Melon.* New York: G.P. Putnam's Sons, 2001.

Moss, Peggy. *One of Us.* Gardiner, ME: Tilbury House, 2010.

Otoshi, Kathryn. *Zero.* San Rafael, CA: KO Kids Books, 2010.

Romain, Trevor. *Cliques, Phonies & Other Baloney.* Minneapolis: Free Spirit, 1998.

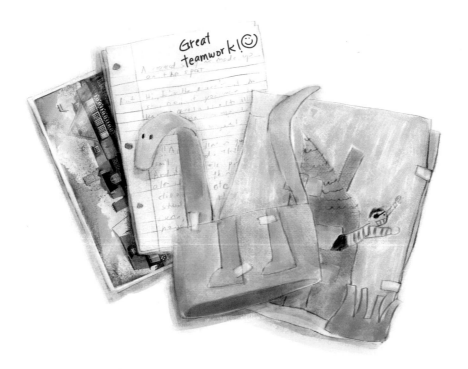

Thank you, Brad, for always including me in your world. —T.J.L.

For Jerry   P.B.

THIS IS A BORZOI BOOK PUBLISHED BY ALFRED A. KNOPF

Text copyright © 2013 by Trudy Ludwig

Jacket art and interior illustrations copyright © 2013 by Patrice Barton

All rights reserved. Published in the United States by Alfred A. Knopf, an imprint of Random House Children's Books,
a division of Random House, Inc., New York.

Knopf, Borzoi Books, and the colophon are registered trademarks of Random House, Inc.

Visit us on the Web! randomhouse.com/kids

Educators and librarians, for a variety of teaching tools, visit us at RHTeachersLibrarians.com

Library of Congress Cataloging-in-Publication Data

Ludwig, Trudy.

The invisible boy / by Trudy Ludwig.

p. cm.

Summary: Brian has always felt invisible at school, but when a new student, Justin, arrives, everything changes.

ISBN 978-1-58246-450-3 (trade) — ISBN 978-1-58246-451-0 (lib. bdg.) — ISBN 978-0-449-81820-6 (ebook)

[1. Popularity—Fiction. 2. Friendship—Fiction. 3. Schools—Fiction.] I. Title.

PZ7.L9763Inv 2013

[E]—dc23

2012042631

The illustrations in this book were created using pencil sketches painted digitally.

MANUFACTURED IN MALAYSIA

October 2013   10 9 8 7 6 5 4 3 2 1   First Edition

Random House Children's Books supports the First Amendment
and celebrates the right to read.